THE BOOK OF THE FILM

Martin Howard

WALKER
ENTERTAINM

CHAPTER ONE

THE COCKEREL CROWED.

In the barn, Shaun the Sheep opened one eye. Another day on Mossy Bottom Farm and, as usual, a bungling spider was caught in its own sticky strands in the beams above his head. Shaun stretched and peered at his reflection in the mirror. The sheep were overdue a shearing, and his wool was long and bedraggled. Working

3

quickly, he ruffled it into a funky style, then gave himself a wink and a thumbs-up. He was looking *good*.

In the farmhouse, the Farmer's alarm clock went off in his bedroom: *ding-a-ling-a-ling*! A pyjama-clad arm shot out and thumped it. With a yawn, a bleary-eyed Farmer sat up in bed. Peering at his bedside table, he tore a page from his calendar. "MONDAY" became "TUESDAY". In the bathroom, the Farmer stared at his groggy reflection and groaned. Reaching for his razor, he began to shave.

Outside, the Farmer's trusty sheepdog, Bitzer, peered out of his kennel and tucked a newspaper under one arm. Grabbing a roll of toilet paper, he set off for his favourite tree. When he had finished, he hurried over

to the farmhouse, where he polished the Farmer's Wellington boots and arranged them neatly by the door. Bitzer saluted as the door crashed open … and smashed into his nose. The Farmer, oblivious, strode past towards the barn.

Bitzer shuffled out from behind the door and followed.

The Farmer threw open the barn door and plucked the day's schedule from its nail, peering at it through thick glasses while Bitzer blew his whistle for the sheep to line up. A particularly loud *peeeeeep* shrieked in Shaun's ear. He glared and stuck a hoof into the whistle, silencing it. Bitzer gave him a dark look before running ahead of the Flock as they traipsed out of the barn and across the farmyard towards the main gate. Bitzer was already there, a sign in his paw with a flattened glove stuck to it: STOP. The Farmer pushed the gate open. After checking that the road was clear, Bitzer turned his sign. Another glove pointed towards the meadow on the other side of the road: GO. The Flock began to cross.

Shaun looked around as they trotted across the road. Mossy Bottom Farm was waking up. On the pond, ducks were quacking – complaining that their bread delivery was late – while yawning pigs leaned against a wall.

Peeping on his whistle again, Bitzer herded the Flock towards the feeding troughs. When the sheep had finished their breakfast, he led them towards a small pen.

Shaun squeezed into the tiny space with the rest of the sheep, holding his breath as the Farmer swung the gate shut and latched it with a grunt of effort.

Shaun bleated. The Flock was packed so tightly he couldn't touch the ground with his hooves.

The Farmer didn't notice, already striding back across the meadow. In the shed, he pushed aside a forgotten photograph that had been taken years before, after a picnic in the meadow on a sunny spring day. In the centre was the Farmer – younger and with much more hair. On one side of him stood Bitzer, on the other, Shaun. The rest of the Flock was lined up behind, eyes twinkling with fun and a grin on every face.

The Farmer ignored it. "Ah-ha," he

mumbled to himself when he found what he was looking for. Whistling, he strode back across the grass, opened the pen and waded into the crowd of sheep, a set of clippers in his hand. With a flick of his thumb, he turned them on. Startled sheep reared back at the buzzing sound.

Shaun groaned to himself. He *hated* shearing time. Seeing a chance for escape, he ducked between the Farmer's legs and made a break for it.

"Gaargh!" shouted the Farmer, grabbing at him. Shaun bleated, his legs whirling. He was free … free…

The Farmer's hand shot out and grabbed Shaun by his straggly wool. The escape was over.

Locked between the Farmer's legs, Shaun winced and made faces while his wool was clipped away. When the Farmer had finished, the pigs pointed and jeered, squealing with laughter at Shaun's new haircut. Turning, he gave the Farmer a grim look.

Lost in a cloud of flying wool, with the next sheep already between his legs, the Farmer didn't even notice.

By the time Bitzer herded the cropped Flock back to the barn, the grey sky was darkening. Shaun looked on as the Farmer wrote out the next day's schedule and then reached to pull the barn door closed behind him. For an instant, the Farmer was silhouetted against the sunset, the red

glow making him look dark and sinister. Shaun blinked, then turned to peer at the timetable. Tomorrow would be another day packed with not-much-fun.

Clunk. The barn door bolted shut.

Shaun lay down in his straw bed, the sounds of the Flock settling around him. Another day over. With a heavy sigh, he closed his eyes.

THE COCKEREL LOOKED UP at another grey sky, shrugged, lifted a megaphone to his beak and crowed.

As the Flock groaned awake, Shaun opened his eyes to see the same spider in the same web on the same beam. In the farmhouse, the Farmer knocked his alarm clock onto the floor, sat up and tore another day off his calendar. "TUESDAY" became "WEDNESDAY". In his kennel, Bitzer reached for the newspaper.

Hearing the rumble of a passing bus, Shaun glanced out of the window, and stared. A large advert had been pasted along the side of the bus. It read: "HAVE A DAY OFF!"

The words gave him an idea: a *good* idea. *A day off*, he thought to himself. A day off. A day off from the dull routine of Mossy Bottom Farm. A day lying back in a sun-lounger, eating ice cream, and sipping an exotic drink from a glass loaded with fruit and a tiny umbrella.

A smile spread across his face.

With an urgent bleat, Shaun called the rest of the Flock into a huddle. The sheep began to giggle.

Moments later, the barn door creaked open. Shaun peered towards the farmhouse. Through the bathroom window he could see the Farmer. Meanwhile, Bitzer squatted under his favourite tree, hidden behind the pages of his newspaper.

The coast was clear.

On tiptoe, Shaun pushed a wheelbarrow to the gate, then made his way to a dark alley between two outbuildings. A shifty-looking duck was waiting. In quiet bleats, Shaun explained what he wanted, holding out slices of bread.

The duck looked from side to side, making sure they weren't being watched, then counted the slices. He shook his head: the payment was unacceptable.

With a sigh, Shaun counted out a few

more slices and handed them over. Help from ducks did not come cheap.

Taking the bread from Shaun's hoof, the duck counted his stack again and folded the slices with a nod. Shaun had bought himself a favour.

Shaun rubbed his hooves together: now all he had to do was move the scarecrow.

A little while later, he pulled the barn door closed behind him. Everything was ready.

Bitzer leaned on his kennel, sipping a mug of tea, and enjoying a few moments of peace and quiet. With the mug halfway to his mouth, he started suddenly, slopping his drink. His eyes grew wide.

In the grass, just ahead of him, was a large, juicy bone.

A bone that was begging to be chewed.

Bitzer's heart began to pound. It was a beautiful bone. And it was calling to him. Nothing else existed. It was just him and the sweet, sweet bone.

Dropping his mug, he leapt at it.

The bone twitched, and jerked away.

With a whuff of surprise, Bitzer jumped again. This time, the bone skipped into the air before shooting away again. Growling in frustration, Bitzer gave chase.

In the bushes, the duck quacked quietly to itself. The plan was working! The duck flapped away and the long piece of string tied to its tail feathers pulled tight. At the other end, the bone jumped out of Bitzer's grasp once more. Drooling, and completely mesmerized, the sheepdog followed the bone as it jumped and jerked across the farmyard.

Meanwhile, at the farmhouse door, the Farmer whistled and looked around grumpily for his sheepdog. Bitzer failed to appear. Grumbling and tutting to himself, the Farmer walked to the barn. He pulled the door open with a yank, then stepped back in surprise. The Flock were perfectly lined up before him, with Shaun front and centre. The sheep stared up at him with innocent eyes.

Puzzled, and still muttering about Bitzer's mysterious absence, the Farmer led the sheep over to the gate, where he bent over to release the latch. At the same time, Shaun hooked a rubber band between his hooves and pulled it tight with a piece of folded paper. One eye closed, he took careful aim…

TWANG!

The paper missile zipped across the farmyard and hit the back of the Farmer's head. Yelping, he stood up straight and rubbed it, looking around. Behind him, the sheep stood in a perfect line, faces radiating innocence. As one, they pointed towards the gate as if to say, "It was *him*."

The Farmer's gaze followed the pointing hooves, and he stared in disbelief.

The scarecrow stared back.

The Farmer blinked and stared some more. It just wasn't possible…

Behind him, Shaun gestured to the rest of the Flock: *move it!*

As escaping sheep streamed past him, the Farmer shouted, sprinted ahead of them and skidded to a halt in front of the charging Flock, holding up a hand.

The plan was working perfectly! Shaun tried his best to put an apologetic look on his face as he and the rest of the Flock trudged back to the gate. With a glance over his shoulder to make sure the Farmer was watching closely, Shaun tensed his muscles and jumped. Landing on all fours on the other side of the gate, he trotted away.

The rest of the Flock followed suit. One by one, sheep jumped the gate while the Farmer counted to make sure that none had escaped.

One … two … three…

Twenty-six … twenty-seven…

Forty-three … forty-four…

The Farmer yawned. There seemed to be more sheep than usual, and he was feeling strangely sleepy. He must have made a mistake, he told himself … fifty-eight … fifty-nine … but he couldn't stop counting…

The Farmer's drooping eyelids jerked open. Had he seen the same sheep twice?

Seventy-eight … seventy-nine …

His eyes began to close again.

Shaun scrambled through a hole in the hedge and joined the end of the queue waiting to jump again. Hearing a loud yawn, he looked round to see the Farmer topple backwards into the wheelbarrow.

For a second, it looked like he might wake up. Shaun watched nervously, and let out a whistle of relief when the Farmer snuggled into the wheelbarrow and began to snore.

The old counting-sheep trick had worked! With the Farmer sleeping like a baby, the Flock could enjoy a day off!

A cheer broke out. Turning, Shaun shushed the Flock. *Don't wake him!*

The sheep nodded in agreement and shushed each other. Young Timmy blinked up at Shaun in awe. It was a *great* plan. Shaun was a genius!

Patting the little lamb on the head, Shaun bleated softly. Before the Flock could relax, there were a few loose ends to tie up. They knew what they had to do. Sheep nodded

and scurried away. A few seconds later, a pair of noise-cancelling headphones was whipped out of the tractor cab while hooves plucked a clean pair of pyjamas from the washing line.

Bitzer, meanwhile, jumped up at the bone hanging from a branch above him. On the other side of the tree, the bored duck yanked on his string. For the umpteenth time, the bone bounced out of the sheepdog's reach.

Back at the gate, the Flock dressed the snoring Farmer in the pyjamas, and slipped the headphones over his ears. Bleating in whispers, they pushed the wheelbarrow across the farmyard and over the fields. There, in a forgotten corner of Mossy Bottom Farm, was a half-rusted caravan that hadn't been used for years, rotten logs jammed beneath its wheels to stop it moving.

Shaun pulled the door open and gestured to the Flock. Hooves lifted the Farmer gently and carried him inside. Carefully, the sheep lowered him onto a bed and draped him with a blanket. Shaun removed the Farmer's glasses and balanced them on a shelf by the door.

The Farmer smiled through his snores, nestling into the blanket.

A hoof to his lips, Shaun pulled down the dark-blue blind at the window. There was just one thing left to do. With a piece of chalk, Shaun drew a moon and stars on the blind and stuck the chalk back in his fleece. Now, if the Farmer woke up, he'd look at the window and think it was the middle of the night.

Giggling, the Flock filed out, leaving the Farmer to his dreams. Beneath their hooves, the old caravan shifted slightly on the rotten logs. Gleefully looking forward to their day off, none of the sheep noticed.

Outside, hooves slapped together in excited high-fives. With the Farmer tucked up safe and cosy, Shaun led the frolicking sheep back across the fields. He scrunched up the day's schedule and kicked it into the sky. It landed at the feet of Mowermouth the goat, who ate it.

The day off could begin. Inside the farmhouse, Timmy trampolined on the sofa while sheep scrambled into the kitchen. Shaun stuffed flowers into the blender to make a smoothie. Someone opened the microwave door and pushed the "ON" button, holding a bag of popcorn on a fork inside to heat it up. The microwave crackled, then exploded, sending the fork shooting across the kitchen to stick into the wall. Another sheep bent a frozen pizza in half and stuffed it into the toaster. Yet another settled into a chair and began flicking through the Farmer's magazines. They were all about farming: *boring*. As one of the sheep, Nuts, scrabbled to reach the ice cream on the top shelf of the freezer, the door swung closed behind him. A few moments later, hooves pulled it open again. A Nuts-shaped ice block fell out.

Eventually, however, the entire Flock gathered in front of the TV in the lounge.

With a grin, Shaun picked up the remote control and bleated: *what should they watch first?* A Western!

From the doorway behind him, Shaun heard a growl. With a gulp, he dropped the remote and turned.

Holding a duck under one arm, Bitzer glared at him.

CHAPTER THREE

BITZER GROWLED: *where was the Farmer?*

Shaun sighed. His plan had been well and truly busted.

Bitzer growled again. He was waiting…

Shaking his head in disappointment, Shaun led him out of the front door, across the fields and back to the caravan. The sheepdog stood on tiptoe to peer in through a tiny crack at the bottom of the blind, and whuffed in shock as he spotted the sleeping Farmer. What had the sheep done? Dashing to the door, he yanked the handle.

It was stuck.

He whuffed furiously at Shaun and pulled harder.

The caravan shifted. With a damp *crunch* of rotten wood, the logs beneath its wheels collapsed.

The door handle ripped away in Bitzer's paw. A shocked silence fell, interrupted only by the creaking of a rusty old caravan on the move.

The Flock stared, wide-eyed, their heads turning slowly as the caravan rolled towards the gate.

With a yelp, Bitzer dashed after the

runaway vehicle. He dived, paws reaching for the bumper, while the sheep gave chase, grabbing at Bitzer's ankles.

Dragging Bitzer and the Flock through the mud, the caravan squeaked and rumbled across fields until the bumper came away in Bitzer's paws. The sheep and sheepdog lay sprawled in the muck.

Freed of the extra weight, the caravan shot forward. Bitzer struggled out from beneath a heap of sheep, and he watched the caravan smash through the farm gate, hit a rock, and turn, bouncing away down the road. It disappeared over the horizon.

The bent bumper dropped from Bitzer's paws. With his tongue lolling out, he set out along the road, past a signpost that pointed to the Big City. The caravan careered through a set of traffic lights and streaked along the road, knocking aside a cow and sending it jumping over a sign for The Moon pub. Ears streaming behind him, Bitzer groaned as the lights turned from green to red. For a few moments, he waited, whistling a nervous tune, then sprinted forward as they flashed back to green.

Ahead was a steep hill. Bitzer felt a surge of hope – the caravan was slowing as it climbed the slope. He could catch it! Gritting his teeth, he put on a fresh spurt of speed.

By the time the caravan reached the top of the hill, it had almost, but not quite, squeaked to a stop. Bitzer's paws reached for it, but were a second too late. The caravan rolled onto the downward slope and began to pick up speed again. Bitzer could only stare after it in dismay. In the distance ahead were the skyscrapers of the Big City, and the caravan was speeding straight towards them!

Sheep panted to a stop around him, gazing down the hill as the caravan became a small, fast-moving dot. With an angry growl, Bitzer pointed a paw back towards the farm. The Flock had done enough damage for one day. He would follow the caravan alone.

Puffing as he ran, Bitzer watched aghast as a red barrier came down across the road in front of the zooming caravan. A loud warning bell rang: *DING-A-LING-A-LING.*

It sounded almost like an alarm clock.

The caravan crashed through the barrier

and trundled across the railway crossing. Wheels jolted and the catch on the window blind snapped. Shaun's drawing of a moon and stars flapped briefly as the blind rolled back. Sunlight streamed into the caravan.

Half a second later, a massive train shrieked past, missing the caravan by inches.

DING-A-LING-A-LING.

Inside the caravan, a hand shot out from beneath a blanket and thumped an old alarm clock from the bedside table. Yawning, the Farmer sat up. The ear protectors slipped off his head and dropped behind a pillow. Grumpily, he clambered out of bed and scratched his bottom. Reaching out, he tore a leaf from a farming calendar, too sleepy to notice that it was fifteen years out of date. He also failed to notice that instead of a view of Mossy Bottom Farm from his bedroom window, there was a view of a busy road.

The Farmer looked into the window, thinking it was his bedroom mirror. Alongside, he saw only the side of a lorry, which was carrying an advert for men's hair gel. Picking up a can of insect repellent, the Farmer sprayed his armpits and peered into the face of a square-jawed male model, surprised by how good he was looking this morning. It was all the healthy, outdoor living that kept him so youthful. Grinning, he gave himself a thumbs-up. *Still got it*, he thought. Clutching a dusty curtain, he mopped his face and turned away just as the lorry pulled past. The "mirror" became a view of buildings on the outskirts of the city. Cars swerved past, drivers honking their horns.

The Farmer's face froze in shock. Eyes popping out of his head, he gave a strangled yell as understanding dawned. This wasn't his bedroom. Somehow, he was in an out-of-control caravan, tearing along a busy road straight towards a large building, which was getting closer – much closer! With another yelp, he dropped to the floor, pulling his knees up to his chest and clutching his head, babbling to himself in shock as he waited for the crash.

Instead, the turning of the caravan's rusty axles finally slowed as the vehicle rolled up a gentle incline. With a squeaky bump, it hit a kerb and stopped completely.

The Farmer opened his eyes. He was safe! With a sigh of relief, he clambered to his feet and pushed the door open. It slammed into a Belisha beacon.

On top of its pole, the beacon's flashing orange globe wobbled dangerously as the Farmer stepped out into the city, blinking behind his thick glasses. With a thump, the beacon dropped onto the caravan's roof and rolled down with a faint rumble.

Bonk – the heavy orange globe hit the Farmer on the head.

Slowly, he toppled backwards with a peaceful smile on his face and birds tweeting around his head: out cold.

A woman screamed and reached for her mobile phone...

Minutes later, Bitzer arrived and stared

at the caravan, which was now surrounded by a large crowd. He scurried forward, pushing his way through the mass of people, his desperate whuffs drowned out by the wailing of an ambulance siren. Before he could get to the Farmer, doors slammed shut and the ambulance sped away.

For a second, Bitzer gazed after it in dismay. Then, gathering his strength once more, he dashed after it.

CHAPTER FOUR

THE MISERABLE SHEEP slowly shuffled through the shattered remains of the farm gate. Last in was Nuts. As he wandered past the "PLEASE SHUT THE GATE" sign, he pulled the gate closed behind him. What was left of it groaned and fell off its hinges.

Ahead, at the farmhouse, Shaun stared forlornly through the window, while the Flock clustered around him. Angry bleats filled the air as they peered in. The farm-house was shaking to loud music. Half-eaten food had been trodden into the carpet. Spilled drinks dripped onto the floor.

While the Flock had been chasing the caravan, the pigs had taken over the farmhouse. One of them boogied past the window; he was dressed in the Farmer's underpants, wellies and hat. Noticing the sheep staring at him, he yanked the curtains closed.

With a sad shake of his head, Shaun tore his gaze away from the curtains and bleated, hopefully. The Flock could still enjoy the day off, they'd just have to do it outside. Carrying a deckchair from the shed, he set it up by the sheep dip and stepped back: *ta-da*, a day at the pool!

The sheep looked at him, then up at the miserable grey sky, then at each other. One by one, they wandered away to nose at an empty feed bag, then looked back at Shaun. With the Farmer gone, there was no one to feed them. What were they supposed to eat and drink?

Stumped, Shaun looked around the farmyard. As his gaze settled on the tractor, an idea flashed into his mind: he could go after the Farmer and bring him back! Quickly, he scrambled up into the driver's seat, and pushed at levers and buttons. The tractor clattered to life. With a grin, Shaun pulled a lever. The tractor gave a whine, and lurched backwards through a hedge, Shaun clinging desperately to the steering wheel. Churning great tracks in the mud, and with Shaun bleating wildly, the tractor smashed through the gate of the bull's field. Snorting furiously, the bull lowered his horns and gave chase across the farmyard. Sheep scattered. Shaun turned the wheel. The tractor swerved and crashed through Mowermouth's pen. The goat stared as the tractor rumbled past and knocked over the hen house. Chickens blinked in the sudden sunlight, squawking angrily after the speeding tractor.

While chaos descended on Mossy Bottom Farm, two doctors and a nurse looked down at the Farmer, who was lying in bed, a bandage around his head, a hospital bracelet on one wrist and a forkful of hospital food in his hand.

"Hoi!" the Farmer squawked in annoyance as the nurse pulled his half-finished dinner away. Ignoring him, doctors bent over, flashing lights in his ears and eyes. The older doctor tapped the Farmer's elbow with a small hammer. The whole arm jerked, flinging the Farmer's fork across the room, where it knocked a picture off the wall.

The doctor murmured to himself. Walking to the end of the bed, he lifted a clipboard. Beside a photo of the Farmer were the words "NAME: MR X". Below, it read, "PROBLEM: MEMORY LOSS."

"Ah hum," said the second doctor, pulling a set of flash cards from a packet and holding them in front of the Farmer, one after the other. Did any of them remind him of his own job?

The Farmer peered through his glasses at pictures of a construction worker, fireman, office worker, a judge wearing a long wig...

He shook his head.

The doctor held up another card. This time the picture showed a man next to a tractor on a farm. Did it jog his memory?

The Farmer looked carefully, and shook his head: *no.*

The doctors muttered to each other. It was a difficult case. "Needs more tests," the younger doctor scribbled on the chart. The older doctor brightened, and swung his arms: *golf?*

He shot the Farmer an encouraging smile and bustled away, the junior doctor and nurse close behind.

*   *   *

Back on the farm, Shaun climbed down from the tractor and stumbled dizzily across the farmyard. By now, some of the sheep were clutching at the Farmer's clothes, weeping. They scowled at Shaun and filled his ears with furious bleats. This was all *his* fault. If it weren't for Shaun and his stupid plans, everyone would be fed and watered and happily grazing in the meadow. Shirley, the largest of the sheep, grabbed the Farmer's wellies and hugged them to her chest, sobbing.

Stamping a hoof, Shaun rolled his eyes. All he'd done was try to give everyone a nice day off!

With a growl of engine and a hiss of

opening doors, a bus pulled up to the lane beside Mossy Bottom Farm. Shaun glanced at it. Across the side of the bus was another advert. This one said: "GET GOING."

Nodding to himself, Shaun turned and stomped away.

The Flock watched him disappear into the shed. A moment later, they peered in to see Shaun rummaging through piles of junk. Pulling out an old satchel, he started filling it: toy binoculars; a piggy bank rattling with coins; the old cassette tape deck that the Farmer used to take on picnics. Pausing, he picked up the dusty photograph of the young Farmer with Bitzer and the Flock. It was just what he needed. He took it out of its frame and added it to the satchel.

Surrounded by blinking sheep, Shaun strolled out of the shed with the satchel slung over one shoulder, then ran for the bus stop.

The Flock followed, watching in surprise as he crept onto the bus and scrambled up to the top deck while the driver was busy changing the destination board to read "THE BIG CITY". Taking a seat at the front, Shaun retrieved the photo from his satchel and tore out the picture of the Farmer. He pulled a pencil from his backpack and scribbled a word across the top: "MISSING". Then he pressed the image against the window to show the sheep gazing up at him from the side of the road.

The doors closed with a hiss. The bus

pulled away. Shaun was off to find the Farmer. He pressed "PLAY" on the tape deck, smiling to himself as he listened to the familiar, tinny tune that came from it.

In the lane behind, the Flock broke into a cheer.

CHAPTER FIVE

FACE PRESSED UP against the window, Shaun watched as tall skyscrapers, bill-boards, bright lights and graffiti whizzed past. The bus roared into the heart of the city and into a crowded station, where it shuddered to a stop. Hearing the doors below open, Shaun scrambled beneath a seat and waited for the bus to empty before scampering down the stairs.

Putting his nose around the door, Shaun was about to step down into the bus station when he stopped. Beneath a sign that read "CITY DRY CLEANERS", a small and hungry-looking stray dog poked her head into a rubbish bin and started to rummage for food. She looked up and, catching Shaun's eye, smiled a crooked smile.

A man in uniform strode across the bus station and strung crime scene tape around the dog's bin. Shaun narrowed his eyes, taking in the words "Officer Trumper" and "City Animal Containment Unit" on his jacket. The man snapped a photo of the little dog and dragged her away by the scruff of her neck. After throwing the dog into the back of his truck, Officer Trumper pulled a clipboard from the dashboard and began to fill out an official form. Across the top of the photograph he stamped the word "CONTAINED".

A bus pulled into the station and grumbled to a stop beside Shaun. A flash of white caught the corner of his eye. Taking his eyes off Trumper, he glanced up … and gasped.

Timmy waved down from the top deck of the newly arrived bus. He was soon joined by another sheep, then another. Before long, the entire Flock was waving at Shaun. Shirley bleated: *we came too!*

Shaun stared at the sheep, and then at Trumper, then back at the Flock. They had to get out of the bus station, *fast*! Shaun waved at the sheep frantically. Grinning and bleating, they scrambled down the stairs and piled out onto the station's floor.

Several metres away, Trumper stopped writing. His ears twitched. Was that *bleating* he heard? *Sheep* bleating?

Trumper looked up just as the last fluffy white tail disappeared behind a bus. His senses twanged, and he hadn't become the city's number one Animal Containment Officer by ignoring twanging senses. Something was going on, and he was going to find out what.

Setting down his clipboard, Trumper stalked across the station and looked around.

Nothing.

Suddenly, he dropped into a crouch. Then he stood, holding something up to his eyes: a small wisp of fleece. He looked around again, his gaze passing over a poster advertising countryside holidays. The lovely picture showed sheep gambolling across rolling hills.

As Trumper looked away, Shaun took a deep breath. Gesturing at the Flock to stay quiet, he crept away into a shopping arcade. The Flock followed, leaving the countryside landscape empty of sheep.

Turning again, Trumper's eyes narrowed. The poster looked different somehow. He took a step forward and spied a fluffy tail disappearing into a charity shop called "ANIMAL HELP". He took another step, and another, his pace quickening as he strode towards the shop. Shouting, he broke into a run.

Inside the shop, Shaun pointed desperately at a rack of old clothes. Hooves reached out and grabbed whatever was nearest.

With a small cry of triumph, Trumper wrenched open the door, flashing an official badge with his free hand.

The cry died in his throat. He blinked. There were no animals in the shop, just a strange-looking family of four – a mum and dad with two sons, a young schoolboy and a hulking teenager. All of them were dressed in a jumbled assortment of mismatched clothes. The only animal he could see was a backpack in the shape of a baby lamb that the teenager was wearing.

Trumper stepped aside as the family turned to leave. He blushed and shuffled his feet nervously as he caught the mother's eye; he couldn't help noticing that the woman was rather attractive. With a cough, he tapped her on the shoulder as she passed by.

The woman turned slowly, staring Trumper in the face.

Giving her a wink, he handed her a handbag. She had been about to leave it behind.

She nodded – *thanks* – and hurried through the door after her family, leaving Trumper in an empty shop.

With Shaun – dressed as the schoolboy – in the lead, the Flock walked away as fast as they dared, following the "lady" – the sheep Twins, one atop the other. Beneath smelly old clothes, Nuts sat on Shirley's shoulders. They were the "dad", while a sheep named Hazel and Timmy's Mum were dressed as the teenager, with Timmy clinging to them as a novelty backpack.

At the bus station's wide entrance, the Flock family lurched to a halt. Spread out before them was the city, all noise and lights and giant advertisements and horn-hooting traffic and rumbling buses. A vast swarm of humans jostled and pushed their way through the streets. The air was full of shouts, exhaust fumes and the smell of hot dogs cooking.

The Flock took it all in. They weren't on Mossy Bottom Farm any more.

CHAPTER SIX

BITZER STAGGERED to a halt by the ambulance, now parked, and mopped sweat from his brow. Ahead, a glass door slid open: the hospital. With a determined puff, he ran up the steps and through the sliding door...

A second later, he came back through it, backwards. As his backside hit the pavement, the security guard who had thrown him out stabbed a finger at a sign: "NO DOGS".

Bitzer watched the door slide closed, then slunk away to sit on a nearby bench. What could he do now? The Farmer must be somewhere inside the hospital and Bitzer had to find him. He glanced towards the hospital door. The guard was still frowning at him through the glass.

Bitzer's head turned at the sound of squeaking wheels. A laundry trolley was approaching, a hospital porter's red face just visible over the top. It stopped by Bitzer's bench while the porter took a puffing breather, then creaked onwards towards the hospital entrance.

Squeak, squeak, squeak… The laundry

trolley approached the door. It hissed open. With a nod, the security guard stepped aside to let it pass and the trolley trundled off down a corridor. He looked towards the bench and noted that the dog had finally gone.

Inside, the porter took another quick break, then the trolley squeaked away again. It left behind Bitzer, now dressed in green surgical scrubs, a hat and a face mask. With a snap, he pulled on a pair of rubber gloves. He looked around nervously, then pulled the face mask down, his nose twitching. He caught the Farmer's scent, and dashed down the corridor.

A few minutes later, Bitzer peered round a door. His eyes lit up. On a bed, happily scoffing from a tray of food, was the Farmer.

Voices echoed down the hallway. Bitzer turned to see two doctors and a nurse heading towards him. The sheepdog whuffed in frustration. He was so close; he couldn't get caught now. Quickly, he pulled up his mask and strode down the corridor. He peered up at a noticeboard, trying to look like any other doctor and hoping they would turn off into a room.

They didn't. From the corner of his eye, Bitzer saw they were still walking straight towards him. He gulped, turned away, then gulped again as two security guards appeared at the other end of the corridor. He was trapped between the two groups. Quickly, Bitzer took the only escape route left. Stepping backwards through a door, he pushed it open with his bottom. A sigh of relief escaped his mouth as the door swung closed. That had been close...

A voice behind him called out.

Bitzer spun round. Dressed, like him, in surgical scrubs and masks, several members of hospital staff looked up from washing their hands and nodded. On the other side of the room, a patient lay on an operating table, surrounded by complicated-looking machines and trays of sharp instruments. A nurse entered, forcing Bitzer further into the operating theatre. Another held a set of medical notes before Bitzer's eyes.

Bitzer took one look and almost threw up over the gruesome pictures. He looked up at the nurse with fear in his eyes. The hospital staff thought he was the surgeon!

And they were preparing the patient for him. After glancing at the notes, he scuttled backwards to the sink and removed his gloves. He held his paws under the tap, thinking furiously. What could he do now?

His thoughts were interrupted by a scream.

Bitzer whipped round. On the operating table, the patient had seen Bitzer's tail hanging beneath the hem of his medical gown. The man started to yell, but the sound was muffled by a mask one of the doctors had quickly clamped over his mouth. The team of medical staff held the struggling man down until he slumped into unconsciousness.

Impatiently, the medics turned to Bitzer. The patient was ready.

Bitzer looked around nervously. There was no escape. He would just have to do the operation. After all, how difficult could it be? He snapped his gloves back on.

Heart in his mouth, Bitzer shuffled towards the patient. He glanced up at a diagram of the human body on the wall, hoping it would give him some clues. Reaching out a trembling paw – hidden inside the rubber glove – he grabbed a large saw. Across the table, a nurse's eyes opened wide in shock. She glanced anxiously at the rest of the team, and offered a small scalpel instead.

With a weak laugh, Bitzer dropped the saw back into its tray … and froze.

All thoughts of the operation vanished.

In the corner of the room was a life-size model of a skeleton, hanging from a hook.

Bitzer's mouth began to water. *Bones*, he thought to himself, *so many bones*.

Beneath his surgical mask, he licked his lips.

The promise of bones drove all other thoughts from Bitzer's mind. Whuffing with delight, he leapt across the operating table and fastened his teeth around the biggest leg bone, giving the skeleton a ferocious shake.

The medical team stared in stunned silence for a second before the door banged open again. At an angry shout they turned to see the real surgeon, glaring. What on earth was going on in his operating theatre? Why was a dog dressed in surgical scrubs dragging a skeleton across the room?

*   *   *

61

Moments later, the Farmer peered out of his room. Security guards charged past. An alarm was blaring. He shrugged. Returning to his room, he peered at the clipboard hanging on the end of the bed. "MR X," it said. *Who am I?* he wondered as he scanned the page.

Just then, a man in a white coat walked through the door with a bundle beneath his arm. Setting it on the Farmer's bed, he unrolled it to reveal a set of large and gruesome-looking tools. Humming, he reached for the largest hammer.

The Farmer let out a short shriek. What sort of tests was this doctor going to do with a hammer big enough to break concrete? He didn't wait to find out. Still clutching the clipboard, he fled out into the corridor.

The man in the white coat took no notice. It wasn't his job to look after patients. Raising his hammer, he knocked a nail into the wall, rehung the picture that had been knocked down by the flying fork, then stood back to admire his work.

At the main entrance, the door slid open. The Farmer sneaked out, glancing back over his shoulder nervously. No one was following. Stopping, he looked up and down the street. He had no idea where he was, couldn't remember how he had got there, and had nowhere to go.

CHAPTER SEVEN

SURROUNDED BY a teetering pile of boxes containing umbrellas, glasses, mobile phones, coats, bags and a grumpy-looking old man, the Lost Property lady squinted at the photo Shaun was holding up. She rubbed her chin, shook her head and gestured at the boxes. She couldn't remember anyone bringing the Farmer in, but Shaun was welcome to look. Behind her, the old man peered out of his box.

The Flock – still dressed as a human family – looked around in disappointment. There was no sign of the Farmer, and if he hadn't turned up at the Lost Property office, where could he be?

Turning to leave, Shaun bleated in excitement, pointing at the window. The Farmer had just passed by! Swaying and tottering, the disguised sheep fell out the door and hurried after him.

Ahead, the Farmer walked up to an automatic door. It hissed open. The sheep followed him into a shopping mall, where the Farmer stepped onto an escalator. The sheep staggered after him.

He turned around.

Shaun groaned. It wasn't the Farmer after all – just someone who looked like him. Another man was coming down the escalator on the other side, and he looked like the Farmer, too. Pandemonium broke out on the escalator as jostling sheep hurried down the steps. A few moments later they reached the bottom – in a bleating heap – just in time to see the new Farmer walk past. Up close, he didn't look much like Mossy Bottom's farmer after all.

There! Shaun pointed again. On the other side of a set of glass doors, yet another Farmer walked past. Shaun bleated urgently for the Flock to hurry. This *must* be the real one.

The sheep picked themselves up and rushed for the doors.

Splamm!

Headfirst, the entire Flock slammed into the doors at the same time – looking for a second like flies squashed against a wind-screen – before toppling back. Shaun sat up, rubbing his head. Not all glass doors, it turned out, were automatic.

Next to them, the man pushed open a door and walked past. Once again, his resemblance to the Flock's Farmer vanished up close. Giving the strangely dressed "family" sprawled across the floor a bewildered glance, he walked away.

Back on his feet, Shaun led the Flock family back out onto the street. At the sight of a bald man bending over, he started running again, skidding to a halt when the man stood up. He wasn't bald, just wearing a cycling helmet.

Up ahead was a flashing neon sign in the shape of a sheep. The Flock gasped and gagged as it flickered and changed into a glowing kebab with the word "TASTY" underneath. The thought of food reminded them how hungry they were, though. Staggering to a halt by a stall selling food, Nuts slipped a hoof through the front of the coat that covered him and grabbed a chilli. Stomach rumbling, he took an enormous bite.

A second later, surprised passers-by watched as an odd-looking man in a long coat sprinted towards a fountain. A busking pantomime horse that was dancing between Nuts and the water was ripped in two as the bleating sheep-man shot straight through it and stood at the fountain's edge. More heads turned at the sound of slurping water. A man tutted in disgust, and a woman murmured, "Ooooh, I say," as she walked on with her nose in the air.

Nuts drank deeply, trying to stop the horrible heat burning his mouth, unaware that from behind it looked – and sounded – as though the family's dad was having a pee in the fountain.

Exhausted and disheartened, the Flock finally slumped on a bench. Shaun shook his head. Taking the photo out, he gazed at it, and then looked around. The Big City was *full* of Farmers, Shaun thought glumly to himself.

Ahead, yet another lookalike pushed open a door and disappeared. Perhaps *he* was the Farmer? With no other options, the Flock hurried after him.

As the door swung closed behind Shaun, wonderful smells wafted past his nose and he felt his stomach growl.

The Flock had followed the Farmer lookalike into a restaurant.

The place was full of smartly dressed people. Piano music drifted across the room. The sheep, however, were more interested in the trays the waiters carried at shoulder height, balancing enormous, colourful ice creams, puddings and cakes.

Shaun's tummy rumbled again, the Farmer forgotten. He remembered that he hadn't had so much as a mouthful of grass since waking up. Maybe the Flock could stop here just long enough for lunch…

Behind Shaun, on the pavement outside, the real Farmer wandered past in his pyjamas, looking lost and confused. None of the sheep noticed.

Inside, the head waiter looked the new arrivals up and down. With a sigh, he shook his head slightly, as if saying to himself, "The riff-raff I have to deal with." Forcing a welcoming smile onto his face, he led the bizarre-looking family to a table, where he pulled a chair out and took Shaun's coat.

Taking off her "backpack", Timmy's Mum slid Timmy under the table. The lamb gave an unhappy bleat. Why did *he* have to sit under the table? A glint of mischief sparkled in his eyes. When the waiter tried to push the chair in to seat the Flock family's mum, he pushed back. Frowning, the waiter tried again. And again the chair slid back towards him. While the waiter fought to push the chair into place, Timmy's Mum nudged her son with a hoof. Beneath the table, Timmy sighed, and stopped pushing.

Seated, the Flock looked around the restaurant in fascination. At the next table was a man with perfectly styled hair and a mobile phone held to his ear. He was obviously some kind of celebrity because a gaggle of people were staring at him from outside, their noses pressed against the glass as they waved and took photos.

The waiter returned. The disguised sheep grabbed at the menus he held out.

Shaun stared at the odd book in his hooves. Around him, the other sheep tried to cut up their menus with knives and forks, then looked up at him: *what were they supposed to do?*

Shaun shot a look at the next table, where the celebrity was reading his menu. Copying him, Shaun opened the menu with a flourish. Around the table, the Flock followed his lead.

The celebrity took a sip from his drink. The sheep nodded to each other and did the same.

The celebrity's elbow accidentally knocked a fork from his table. A second later, there was a crash as the sheep all threw their cutlery to the floor.

With a sigh, the head waiter returned to the table to retrieve the fallen knives and forks. At that moment, the celebrity let out a small, polite burp into his fist.

Sheep looked at each other, grinning, and took deep breaths.

Shaun raised his hooves to stop them.

Too late.

The head waiter jumped, yelping as a storm of burps echoed off the walls of the restaurant. Eyes burning with fury, he glared at the family.

Shaun caught a glimpse of Timmy from the corner of his eye. The little sheep had sneaked off to the dessert trolley, which was loaded with delicious cakes. Timmy had already had a taste; his grinning face was covered in cream.

Rolling his eyes, Shaun climbed out of his chair. With one hoof he grabbed Timmy while the other clutched at Timmy's teddy. As he did so, a stray end of wool from his jumper snagged on the trolley.

Not noticing the mess Timmy had made

of the cakes on the lower shelf, a waiter began to push the trolley back towards the kitchen. As it rolled, the trolley pulled the strand of wool on Shaun's jumper. Row after row of knitting unravelled. The last shred caught on Shaun's belt. With a faint *ping*, it pulled the buckle open.

Shaun's trousers fell round his ankles.

Tripping on them, he bleated loudly and threw Timmy into his mum's arms before hitting the floor with a loud crash. By the time he stood, dusting himself down, every pair of eyes in the restaurant was staring at him.

The place had fallen completely silent.

Shaun looked down at himself, and looked up again. His disguise was gone.

The pianist played a loud, crashing chord. The celebrity blinked at Shaun. Across the room, the head waiter's mouth fell open in surprise. A waiter lunged, grabbing for Shaun and breaking the silence with a shout. Suddenly, the air was thick with screams. There was a sheep in the restaurant! Shaun ducked away, and ran for it.

The head waiter grabbed the phone and flicked through a phone book in search of help. With a wave of his fingers, he ordered the pianist to carry on playing, just as Shaun leapt over the piano, a waiter close behind.

Shaun ducked into the kitchen.

A second later, he sprinted out again, a cleaver-waving chef in hot pursuit.

CRASH! He bumped into a waiter holding a tray. The huge fish on it flew off and landed on the celebrity's head. The

celebrity screamed and fell backwards into a lobster tank, where he was promptly attacked by sharp pincers. Struggling to his feet, he ripped a lobster from his nose, tossed it aside and checked his reflection using the back of a spoon. At the sight of his dishevelled hair he screamed again, louder this time. With the head waiter clinging to his arm, he stormed out, clutching his nose and hair.

Just after the celebrity's departure, the menacing figure of Trumper blocked the doorway. A chilling smile crossed his face as he spotted Shaun. His hand held a vicious-looking grabber. The Animal Containment Officer strode across the restaurant and quickly taped off the area. His camera flashed; the word "CONTAINED" was stamped on the picture of a dazed Shaun. With professional efficiency, Trumper fastened the grabber around Shaun's neck and pulled him roughly towards the exit.

As he marched towards the door, Trumper noticed the attractive woman he had seen at the Animal Help shop earlier. He hesitated for a second, shuffling his feet. Then, with a shy smile, he placed his card on the plate in front of her.

A few seconds later, Shaun was bundled into the back of Trumper's van. Shocked and frightened, he peered out of the back window, out into the busy street, and straight into the face of the Farmer.

Shaun's jaw dropped open, and his hooves drummed on the window as the van roared away.

CHAPTER EIGHT

THE CELEBRITY'S LIMO skidded to a stop. Leaping from the driver's seat, the chauffeur pushed an old woman out of the way as he opened the back passenger door.

The celebrity climbed out, glancing around nervously. Head ducked, he ran across the pavement, clutching his ruined hair, and barged through the door of an expensive hair salon.

While the celebrity banged a fist on the reception desk, demanding an emergency restyle, the Farmer wandered up the street. Shuffling to a halt, he stared at his reflection in the salon's window. Inside, the celebrity was ushered into a barber's chair by the manageress, who was wearing a name tag that read "Meryl". Two stylists fussed and buzzed around, prodding the celebrity's hair in horror.

The Farmer blinked. Both stylists wore striped trousers and T-shirts covered in colourful splatters. Plastic festival bracelets hung from their wrists. Around their heads, each sported a headband.

The Farmer looked down at himself. He, too, was wearing stripy trousers. His hospital T-shirt was splattered with colourful

Shaun gets an idea. Let's have a day off!

Shaun shares his plan with Timmy and his mum. They like it.

The sheep jump the fence over and over, to make
the Farmer fall asleep.

The sheep carry the sleeping Farmer to the caravan,
where they'll hide him.

Hooray! A day off!

Time for a party in the Farmer's house!

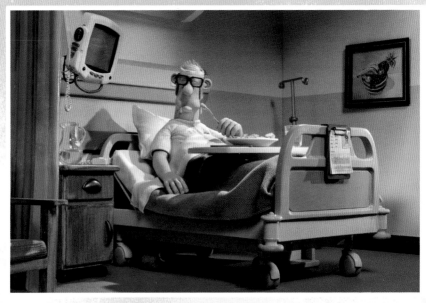

The Farmer wakes up in hospital. He has lost his memory.
He doesn't know who or where he is.

Shaun takes the bus to the Big City to find the Farmer.

The sheep use clothes from a shop to disguise themselves as humans. Trumper doesn't recognize them.

The Sheep eat in a restaurant. Nuts eats the menu.

Shaun and Bitzer are stuck inside the Animal Containment Centre.

The Farmer finds a new way to use his sheep-shearing skills.

Shaun, Bitzer and their new friend, Slip, escape
from the Containment Centre.

Back on the farm, everyone poses for a photo.

splashes of food. Around his wrist was a plastic name-tag bracelet. He put his hand to his head and felt the bandage there.

His gaze fell upon a pair of hair clippers swinging on the back of a chair. There was something about them … something familiar. An image flashed before his eyes: his own hands expertly wielding a pair of clippers.

Unable to take his eyes off the clippers, he drifted towards the door.

The celebrity closed his eyes and breathed a sigh of relief as the two stylists argued back and forth about which one of them should rescue his hair. Across the salon, Meryl barked an order. Obediently, the stylists scurried away from the celebrity and over to their boss.

The door opened and closed.

Unseen by Meryl or the arguing stylists, the Farmer picked up the hair clippers. He was dressed as if he worked in the salon, and the clippers settled snugly into his hand as if he'd used them a thousand times before.

He looked down at the man in the barber's chair.

Eyes still closed, the celebrity clicked his fingers impatiently.

Yes, the Farmer thought to himself. Reaching out, he swung the chair around.

The celebrity blinked his eyes open to see a strange man standing over him with clippers in his hand.

Before he could utter a sound, the

Farmer grabbed him by the scruff of the neck and wrestled him to the floor. Keeping a tight grip, he straddled the celebrity and flicked the clippers on with his thumb. *Oh yes indeed*, the Farmer thought to himself, happily, as hair flew past his ears. He had *definitely* done this before.

Struggling in the Farmer's grip, the celebrity shrieked.

Meryl's high-pitched scream echoed around the salon. Another customer looked up from a magazine, saw what was happening and began to scream, too. At the door, the chauffeur saw his boss pinned to the ground by a clipper-wielding lunatic. His ear-piercing shriek added to the general screeching. An assistant stylist glanced up from washing another customer's hair. Transfixed by the scene, he pushed the woman's head underwater.

The Farmer was almost finished. With a heave, he flipped the celebrity over. Hair flew again as he added a few finishing touches.

The chauffeur grabbed him from behind. Shrugging the man off, the Farmer glanced down at the still-buzzing clippers in his hand, then looked around, dazed.

No one looked back at him. Every pair of eyes in the salon was fixed on the celebrity, whose face twisted in an enraged snarl as he staggered to his feet. He opened his mouth to yell a torrent of abuse … and snapped it shut again.

He had caught a glimpse of himself in the mirror. He leaned closer, turning his head this way and that, and then gasped in delight. His new hairstyle – shaved around the sides with a rounded top – was fabulous!

Breaking into a grin, the celebrity high-fived the Farmer and patted him on the back. He clutched the Farmer round the neck and rubbed his head affectionately. It was a *super* haircut and he *loved* the Farmer's modern technique. Digging a wad of money from his pocket, he pressed it into a surprised Meryl's hands.

The salon burst into applause.

Bemused, the Farmer looked around. Everyone seemed pleased. Slowly, a smile appeared on his face. It got wider when Meryl passed some of the money to him.

The celebrity walked proudly to his limo, turning to shoot a dazzling smile at a fan who was clicking photos with his mobile phone. A few moments later, his car pulled away from the salon, where the Farmer was already working on his next customer.

CHAPTER NINE

SHAUN PEERED THROUGH the window of
Trumper's van, still clutching Timmy's teddy,
his heart sinking as the van reversed through
the entrance of the Animal Containment
Centre. Above the gate, a jolly sign showed
happy animals playing in a sunny field. It
was the only colourful thing Shaun could
see. The building was a grim and grey
prison, surrounded by wire fences. Fixed

to walls and fence posts, security cameras turned slowly, watching every centimetre of the compound.

The van stopped. Shaun blinked as the back doors opened and sunlight streamed in. Nearby, a door buzzed. Trumper dragged him out and into the main building, past cages full of animals. A fierce-looking Rottweiler clutched metal bars, "BARK" and "BITE" tattooed across his paws. A Poodle lay back, bench-pressing a barbell. From the corner of his eye, Shaun saw a cat with a funnel around her neck sniff the air and hiss. Further along, a tortoise slowly scratched a mark on the wall. Shaun noticed there were hundreds of marks already. A goldfish leaned against the glass wall of its bowl, playing a mournful tune on its harmonica.

At last, Trumper stopped, keys clinking, in front of a small cell containing two bunks. Shaun's eyes widened in fear. The cell was already occupied. A dim figure was slumped in the shadows, face to the wall.

With a *clank* and a metallic whine, the door opened. Shaun's pleading bleat was cut off when Trumper shoved him in and slammed the door. After twisting the key in the lock, the Animal Containment Officer strode away with a triumphant smirk.

Shaun turned back to the dim figure with a gulp. The figure stayed where it was, growling quietly.

Shaun squinted, and gave a start, bleating in shocked surprise. The figure stepped into the light, rubbing his growling tummy.

Shaun stared at Bitzer. Bitzer stared back at Shaun.

Shaun couldn't help noticing that the sheepdog did not look pleased to see him. In fact, he seemed downright peeved, shooting Shaun grim looks and muttering to himself. Remembering that if it hadn't been for his big-day-off plan everyone would be safely back at Mossy Bottom Farm, Shaun shuffled his feet, embarrassed. He threw himself onto the spare bunk, watching as Bitzer paced the cell. By now, the sheepdog was whuffing angrily. *If it weren't for Shaun....*

On his bunk, Shaun sighed and stared out through the bars, then gasped in surprise. In the cage opposite was a face he knew – a face that was slightly lopsided.

It belonged to the little dog he had seen being dragged away by Trumper at the bus station. Shaun smiled at her.

The dog, named Slip, gave him a crooked smile in return.

Bitzer was *still* whuffing angrily. Shaun turned, and bleated. It wasn't *all* his fault. He had only been trying to give the sheep a nice day off…

The sheepdog interrupted with a bark. Shaun had come up with some crazy plans before, but this one had landed the whole farm in trouble – especially the Farmer.

While Bitzer and Shaun argued, Trumper returned to his office. He pinned a photo of Shaun to a large board, alongside many other pictures of miserable-looking animals. At the top of the board, large letters spelled out the word "CONTAINED".

Nodding to himself in satisfaction, Trumper turned to face a mirror and drew his grabber the way a cowboy would, holding it towards the mirror. A smile broke out on his face: he was the best Animal Containment Officer in the business.

With a sniff, Shaun folded his arms and looked away from Bitzer. The sheepdog gave a final growl and sat heavily on his bed. Looking up, he saw a face looming above him. A large, creepy-looking dog was staring at him, unblinking.

Bitzer looked away, quickly, and then glanced back. The big dog was still there, eyes fixed on Bitzer.

With a small yelp, Bitzer covered his face with his paws, peering between them.

The creepy dog was still staring.

Somewhere in the distance a door slammed. Shaun jumped as a loud klaxon sounded. What was happening *now*?

He was surprised to see that Slip didn't seem scared. Instead, she licked her paws and smoothed her fur. In the other cages, the rest of the Containment Centre's inmates were combing their coats, hurriedly tying ribbons in their hair and squirting breath-freshener. The tortoise buffed its shell to a shine with an old towel, while the Rottweiler put its tattooed paws behind its back and shuffled its features into a friendly smile. The French Poodle gripped a bone between its teeth in an attempt to look cute. The bone snapped between the dog's powerful jaws.

Shaun squinted along the corridor. By the door, two teenage boys dropped money into a donation bucket. With Trumper looming behind her, a female warden smiled and waved them in. One of the boys picked up an empty pet carrier and followed. A moment later, they stopped by a cage and murmured to each other.

The first boy shook his head and walked on, the warden close behind.

As they came closer, Slip yapped eagerly and fluttered her eyelashes.

With a small cry of delight, the two young people grinned at each other. Shaun saw them nod, happily. They had found their new pet.

Joy broke out on Slip's face and she gave a bark of pure happiness. But it turned into a despairing whine when the two boys walked past her cage.

Passing the goldfish, who fanned herself fetchingly with a seashell, the boys stopped at another cage. The warden reached up, opened the door and dropped an iguana into the shorter boy's arms. Grinning, the boys turned to leave. As they walked away, the iguana leaned over his new owner's shoulder and blew a raspberry at the rest of the inmates.

Scowling, Trumper held two fingers up to his own eyes and then pointed them at the departing iguana. The message was clear: *I'll be watching you.*

Shaun shook his head, sadly, as Slip slunk back into the shadows and curled up. Tears rolled down her peculiar face.

Outside, the sun sank in the sky. Towards evening, the smiley female warden brought food for each of the animals. A little while later, the lights in the Animal Containment Centre went out with a *clunk*. Shaun leaned back against the wall, holding Timmy's teddy tight, wondering what sort of place the city was at night and how the Flock, and the Farmer, would manage without him. The poor man was probably alone and frightened, and it was all his fault...

At that exact moment, far away from the Animal Containment Centre, the fan who had been snapping photos of the celebrity outside the hair salon clicked the mouse of his computer. The pictures he had just taken of the celebrity's new hairstyle appeared on the Internet. Within seconds, they were spreading. Over and over again the words "FABULOUS NEW LOOK" were typed out by amazed style-spotters. The amount of "likes" next to the photos began to increase, speeding up until the numbers began to blur. Before long, a whole new website had gone up. In the centre of its homepage was a picture of the Farmer, surrounded by arty pictures of the sensational new hairstyle he had created. An article appeared: "WHO *IS* MR X?" More coverage followed, complete with posters of the Farmer holding clippers in the shape of an "X", the words "HAIR HERO" beneath. Soon, someone had PhotoShopped his goofy smile into a cool, brooding frown.

At the hair salon, Meryl couldn't answer

the phone fast enough. Every light on the switchboard blinked as more callers tried to get through. Frantically, she scribbled names in the appointment diary while the Farmer gripped yet another customer by the scruff of his neck and swung a leg across his back.

CHAPTER TEN

THE SOUND OF FOOTSTEPS echoed down the grim corridor. In one cell, the Rottweiler and French Poodle looked up in panic. Between them they had dug a large hole in the floor – a hole almost big enough to escape through. Were the two dogs about to make a run for it?

They dropped a bone into the hole and quickly filled it in again. No, they were just being dogs.

Animal Containment Officer Trumper walked slowly past cage after cage, stopping now and again to sneer at the animals inside.

Shaun blinked as Trumper appeared on the other side of the bars.

"Baaa," said Trumper, mockingly.

He turned away and saw Slip gobbling down her bowl of food. Trumper's lip curled as he watched dog biscuits flying everywhere. Pulling a bag of crisps from his pocket, he began to mimic her. Half-chewed crisps sprayed from between his grinding teeth.

Shaun's eyes widened as Trumper leaned over Slip's cage. Hanging from the animal cop's belt was a large bunch of keys.

Quickly, Shaun pressed up against

100

the bars and stretched out a hoof. He could almost touch the keys. Straining, he reached further. Almost, *almost*...

Along the corridor, a buzzer went off. Trumper straightened, watching as the door opened.

Bleating under his breath, Shaun pulled his hoof away and glanced towards the door.

His eyes grew wide in shock.

Standing in the doorway was a figure. A figure with flowing blonde hair and a long coat. A figure that looked very familiar.

The Twins, disguised as the woman, walked towards Trumper, the top sheep smiling sweetly. To one side, a dog sniffed the air and frowned. He realized that the lady swaying down the corridor wasn't a lady! She was an animal, like the inmates. He opened his mouth, his bark turning into a "*whhuu-ump*" as the Twins' handbag hit him in the mouth.

The disguised sheep passed Shaun and Bitzer's cell. The Twin on top shot them a quick look, lips forming a "*shhh*". Taking Trumper by the arm, the sheep-lady pulled him away. Together, they strolled further down the corridor without a backwards glance.

Meanwhile, outside the Animal Containment Centre, the rest of the Flock began Phase Two of the rescue. A sheep held up a banana, and waggled it in front of Shirley's nose. Drooling, she strained towards it, pulling on a rope that had been tied round her shoulders. The other end had been tied to the bars set in a high window.

The rope went tight. The sheep waved the banana again. Sweat popping from her brow, Shirley heaved. There was a grinding sound behind her. The barred window shifted.

The sheep gave the banana one last waggle. Once more, Shirley pulled.

This time the bars came free as the whole wall collapsed onto the pavement below.

With a happy bleat, Shirley leapt at the banana. An alarm went off.

Waaaark-waaaark-waaaark!

The sheep stared at the opening where the wall had just been. There was no sign of Shaun. Instead, caught in the light of a streetlamp, two bank robbers stared back, frozen.

The Flock looked at each other, and bleated: *wrong window.*

Together, they turned. Across the street, Shaun and Bitzer looked down at them from between the bars of the Animal Containment Centre, shaking their heads sadly.

Waaaark-waaaark-waaaark!

Trumper started at the wailing sound and dropped the lady's arm. Head twisting from left to right, he looked round quickly, seeking the source of the alarm. There was an emergency going on and Animal Containment Officer Trumper might be needed…

His thoughts disintegrated as a wet pair

of lips met his in an enormous squelching kiss. Trumper's eyes closed as he kissed the woman back passionately, then snapped open again. There was something very, very wrong with the lady's mouth, including the smell of her breath!

Gagging, he pulled away.

The Twins shoved him in the chest. Trumper stumbled back into a chair and squawked in shock as the attractive woman ran down the corridor, splitting in two as she fled. Still trailing a long coat, wig askew, the Twins shot through the door and away outside.

Realizing he'd been fooled, the Animal Containment Officer rose with a growl. *Someone* was going to pay.

At the same time, an idea popped

into Shaun's head. He still had the chalk he'd used to draw a night-time sky on the caravan's window blind! Quickly, he rummaged around in his fleece until he found it. Now, all he had to do was...

Moments later, Trumper strode down the corridor, his face set in a grim mask. Suddenly, he pitched forward and sprawled across the floor; Slip had poked her leg between the bars of her cell.

Waaaark-waaaark-waaaark!

On his knees, Trumper glanced into Shaun and Bitzer's cell. It was empty. On the far wall was a hole!

Trumper gasped. The alarm had gone off because Shaun and Bitzer were escaping!

Hands trembling, he unlocked the cell door and threw himself inside, reaching into the hole. Then he yelped and jumped back, sucking his stinging fingers.

The hole wasn't a hole. It was a *drawing* of a hole.

Shaun was really quite a talented artist.

Trumper's head turned as the cell door slammed behind him. A key twisted in the lock. He caught a glimpse of Shaun and Bitzer running for the door at the far end of the corridor, releasing animals from their cages as they went. Defeated, Trumper slumped back on the cell's bunk, and looked up. The same scary-looking dog that had been staring at Bitzer was now staring at *him*.

Beneath the streetlights outside, Shaun hugged Timmy and gave him his teddy back. Shaun turned to see Nuts pointing up. There, spread across an enormous advertising billboard was the Farmer's face, with "MR X" written above in huge letters. And in the corner of the advert was a map showing the hair salon's location. A cheer erupted.

Slip bounded onto a dustbin and peered at the map, then whuffed over her shoulder. She knew where the salon was. Did the Flock want to find Mr X?

The sheep nodded back at her eagerly.

Hopping off the dustbin, Slip trotted to a hole in the fence and whuffed at the Flock to follow.

The moon rose higher in the sky as sheep slipped through ventilation ducts and over rooftops, Slip in the lead. Overjoyed that they would soon be reunited with the Farmer, several stopped to dance on the rooftops of old buildings, one sheep so energetically that she dropped down into a chimney and had to be pulled out, covered from head to hoof in soot.

Eventually, the Flock slid down a waste tube on a building site and found themselves on a brightly lit street. Opposite was the hair salon.

The sheep and sheepdog of Mossy Bottom Farm grinned at each other. Through the salon's window was the welcome sight of the Farmer bending over, a pair of clippers in his hand, a customer locked between his knees.

Bleating with joy, Shaun surged forward and bundled through the door. Shrieks split the air. A terrified customer grabbed at the arms of her chair, screaming. Stylists leapt onto another chair, clutching at each other.

In the middle of the chaos, a sheep looked up into the Farmer's face and bleated: *it's me, Shaun!*

The Farmer stared down at him.

Shaun tried a smile.

The smile quickly disappeared as the Farmer coldly shooed him away. Shaun blinked, devastated. Could it be true? Did the Farmer really want him to get lost?

Bitzer's urgent whuffing jolted him out of his trance. Meryl was punching a number into her phone while thrashing at Shaun with a broom. It was time to go. Still staring up at the Farmer, Shaun shook his head. Bitzer grabbed his arm. Hooves squeaked as the sheepdog dragged him across the floor and pushed him out onto the pavement, Meryl close behind.

Shaun barely noticed. He was lost in misery.

CHAPTER ELEVEN

KEYS TURNED in the lock on the cell door. Glowering, Trumper shoved the door open and stomped past the wardens towards his office. Behind him, the two wardens smirked at each other, enjoying the fact that the animals had outwitted the great Officer Trumper.

Throwing open his office door, Trumper crossed the room, past photos of himself posing with various celebrities. His face like thunder, he snatched Shaun and Bitzer's photos from the board that was headed, "CONTAINED", and touched a keypad. Silently, the Contained Board slid back. The other wardens stared, aghast. Behind the secret wall, grabbers stood neatly racked in a line. Every one of them looked horribly cruel. Trumper didn't hesitate. Snatching the most evil-looking contraption from the rack, he flicked a switch. Lights flickered. The machine gave a high-pitched buzz. A small, green picture of an animal turned into a red skull.

Turning, Trumper pointed the machine at a cuddly toy on a shelf and pulled the trigger.

The two wardens dived for cover.

The smoking remains of the toy toppled

over. Beside it, a toy robot whirred into life, putting its hands up in the air. With a satisfied grunt, Trumper stalked out of the room, the Taser clutched tightly in his fist.

Across town, Shaun looked up at the sound of a sharp yap. Further down the street, Slip pushed away a sheet of cardboard to reveal a manhole cover. Opening it, she pointed down.

Meryl's angry shouts still ringing in their ears, the Flock hurried over and peered into the dark hole, bleating anxiously. It was dark down there – and smelly.

Slip yapped again. Stray animals in the city needed to keep out of sight or Trumper would get them. They could use the underground tunnel to escape!

There was nothing else for it. One by one, the Mossy Bottom Farm sheep and sheepdog jumped into the hole. A second later, Slip followed them. Covering the hole with the sheet of cardboard, she breathed a sigh of relief.

Down the drain, it was worse than the pigs' sty, Shaun thought to himself. With sheep sniffing and bleating in disgust, the Flock waded through a stinking stream towards a faint patch of light. At the end of the tunnel, Slip pushed a wire cover to one side. Gratefully, the sheep followed her out, and gazed around at a scene from a nightmare. Slip had led them to a hidden patch of wasteland at the heart of the city, a collection of junk under the graffiti-covered, concrete arches of a flyover.

Unconcerned, Slip led the Flock and Bitzer past old boxes and oil drums and drifting piles of newspapers and filth. A few moments later, they arrived at her home – a kennel made from scraps of cardboard. Next to it was a patch of empty ground where the Flock could sleep.

Shaun blinked, a lump of sadness in his throat. Beside the kennel, Slip had arranged a torn dog-food poster so that she could look out from her rickety home and see smiling, happy people – the kind of owners she would love to have.

The bewildered and frightened Flock drew closer to a fire that burned in a rusty oil drum. This dirty concrete wasteland was so different from their cosy barn and green meadow.

Shaun bleated at them to get some sleep. Dragging a discarded cardboard box onto a pallet, he tried to make a bed. Following his example, all the sheep soon had beds of damp cardboard. Sighing miserably, Shaun lay down on his own, pulling old newspapers over himself. Above, a graffiti cobweb had been scrawled across the underside of the flyover. Shaun stared at it, homesick for the clumsy spider above his own bed back at Mossy Bottom Farm. A tear glistening in his eye, he took out the picture of the Farmer and gazed at it.

From nowhere, a gust of wind caught the old photo. Shaun let it go, tossing it upward. The Farmer no longer cared about them. There was no point in keeping it. The rest of the sheep followed his gaze, watching as the tiny photograph blew away until it was just a dot over the rooftops.

Timmy began to cry. His mother gave him a hug, but it made no difference. His bleating sobs echoed around the arches.

Shaun rummaged in his satchel. Pulling out the old cassette player, he set it on the ground close to the lamb. While the rest of the Flock leaned in, curious, Shaun hit the "PLAY" button.

A voice wafted out of the speaker, filling the night air with music.

Timmy stopped crying. His face brightened and he yawned, lulled into sleepiness by the music … that suddenly slowed down, mangled into gibberish. Words and tune became a horrible cacophony.

As Timmy began to howl again, Shaun

scowled and pulled out the cassette. The ancient machine had chewed the tape. Crushed, he shook his head mournfully. Everything he did went wrong.

Around him, the Flock looked at each other. One by one, they nodded.

Shirley began, bleating a low bass line. Another sheep pulled a ukulele from his fleece and began to strum. The rest of the Flock began to sing, adding harmonies.

Once again, the song wafted out across the wasteland.

Last to join was Nuts. Taking a deep breath, he bleated out a single ear-jangling note.

As the gentle bleating song went on, Timmy settled into his mum's arms again. Soon, his eyelids drooped. And still the sheep sang, their music winding between the tall buildings and drifting across the city.

In the back room of the salon, the Farmer heard faint music. Somewhere deep inside, the beginnings of a memory stirred. He *knew* this song. He looked towards an open window. As the song echoed around the skyscrapers outside, he suddenly felt lost and out of place.

The Farmer blinked as the music stopped. The half-memory vanished. Growling with frustration, he pulled the crumpled medical chart from his pocket and glared at it. Who was Mr X? Where was he supposed to be?

Meryl's voice barked, calling him back to work. With a sigh, the Farmer screwed the chart up, tossed it out the window and turned away.

The scrunched ball of paper disappeared into the night, dropping into a bent drainpipe. A few seconds later, it bounced across a road, down into the wasteland and onto a pile of rubbish.

A hoof picked it up and tossed it at the fire.

Bitzer's nose twitched. A second later, his eyes opened wide as he recognized the familiar scent: the Farmer! With a jerk, he sat up. Where was the smell coming from? His eyes darted this way and that, and finally settled on the ball of paper with flames licking around it.

With a yelp, Bitzer threw himself forward and tried to snatch it from the fire. It was too hot!

In a flash, Shaun grabbed Bitzer's hat. Using it as an oven glove, he pulled the paper from the flames. Bitzer grabbed it. Tossing the burning paper from paw to paw, puffing at it frantically, he managed to put out the flames. Shaking with excitement, he unrolled the charred ball and smoothed it out.

"NAME: MR X

PROBLEM: MEMORY LOSS."

The animals of Mossy Bottom Farm read the words by flickering firelight and gasped.

Shaun's eyes shone with excitement. The Farmer hadn't forgotten them on purpose. He had lost his memory. And he needed to get it back!

What the Flock needed was a plan.

A few minutes later, Shaun tapped a blackboard with a stick. Chalked on the board was "MR X –> MOSSY BOTTOM FARM = FARMER". Once the Farmer was back in his rightful place, his memory would come flooding back. All the Flock needed to do was get him there. Leaning over, Shaun scribbled some more, drawing a picture of the Farmer wearing a helmet.

Sheep sucked in their breath. Bitzer's eyes widened. The plan was bold. It was audacious. It was one of Shaun's best. And, this time, it might just work!

The Flock nodded to each other and went to work. The sounds of sheep rummaging through junk piles rang out in the darkness. Poles bent into strange shapes and a giant spring boinged.

* * *

On the other side of town, Animal Containment Officer Trumper picked a scrap of wool from where it had caught on an old fence. He sniffed at it, his eyes narrowing beneath the hi-tech goggles he was wearing. One hand clenched around the Taser, he raised the other and flicked a switch on the side of his night-vision goggles. He saw the red-tinged outline of a trail of sheep's wool.

They went this way.

Trumper smiled to himself and climbed into his van. He was on the hunt.

CHAPTER TWELVE

AN OLD CAR MIRROR poked around the corner of a dark alley. Reflected eyes peered along the pavement towards the spot where light spilled from the salon window. There was a muffled whuff in the shadows: *all clear.*

Inside the salon, one of the stylists swept at a pile of hair while the other poured coffee. The Farmer groaned, his hand cramped up around the clippers. It had been an exhausting day. He glanced at the clipboard Meryl had hung on the wall. At the top, it read "TOMORROW'S SCHEDULE". The Farmer groaned again and sagged. Every minute of the following day was packed with appointments. It would be the same the day after, and the day after that. He could use a day off.

Hearing a tapping sound, the salon staff looked towards the window. A bizarre sight met their gaze. A small dog with a lopsided face was peering in at them through the glass. Behind her, a gate that looked as though it had been made in a hurry had appeared on the pavement.

Flummoxed, the Farmer, Meryl, and the two stylists stared as a sheep trotted down the road and jumped over the gate. Then another … and another … and another…

A wave of sleepiness swept down the street. The heads of a young couple out strolling dropped, nose-first, into their ice cream cones. In Trampoline World, a salesman dozed off and fell onto one of his products, snoring with every subsequent bounce. A bus swerved down the road, its driver slumped over the wheel.

Meryl's eyes closed. With a yawn, she drifted off to sleep, her head landing on an adding machine. Paper spooled out onto the salon floor.

Leaping over the gate for the third time, Shaun glanced through the window and grinned to himself. The counting-sheep trick never failed. Before Shaun's hooves touched the ground, the Farmer had fallen backwards into a chair, snoring. In fact, Shaun thought as he landed and looked around, it worked a little too well. On the opposite side of the street, the bus veered off the road towards a stack of dustbins...

KERRRR-ASSSHHH!

Quickly, Shaun gave a signal. Sheep stopped jumping and dived into the salon. Lifting the sleeping Farmer out of the door, they carried him into the dark alley. Meanwhile, Bitzer started an engine and put the vehicle the Flock had made into gear.

A moment later, a mechanical panto-mime horse whirred out into the street. Propped on top sat the Farmer, fast asleep, with a helmet on his head. From inside the horse-vehicle, the sheep below held him in place with sticks.

With a grin, Shaun joined the other sheep, elbowing them to make room. When everyone was settled, Shaun peered out through the horse's eye-holes and bleated. Time to go. As Bitzer put the horse into gear, Nuts began clapping two coconut shells together, making clip-clop noises as the fat and lumpy horse skimmed down the road. Shaun grinned to himself. Everything was going to plan…

As they rounded a corner, his grin disappeared.

Boots clumped to a halt on the pavement. Blocking the pantomime horse's path with a raised hand ... was Trumper.

The horse reared backwards, threatening to topple the Farmer. Quickly, the sheep manoeuvred their sticks until he was sitting upright again.

The Animal Containment Officer narrowed his eyes, glaring suspiciously at the strange man on the ragged pantomime horse. Some sort of street performer, he guessed. Then, he held up pictures of Shaun, Bitzer and Slip – the word "CONTAINED" stamped across the top of each one.

Inside the horse, sheep pushed and pulled on their sticks, making the Farmer move like a puppet. His head slumped forward and back in a sloppy nod. His arm rose, pointing back the way the pantomime horse had come.

Trumper growled thanks and stepped aside to let the horse continue on its way. Still suspicious, he turned to watch it go. It was then that he noticed a trail of what looked like wool – and it was coming from the horse! What was going on in there?

Trumper stuck his head into the horse's backside to find out. For a second, there was a stunned silence. The Animal Containment Officer stared in shocked surprise at sheep working the sticks that held the Farmer in place, and Bitzer at the pulleys and levers.

Taking a deep breath, Trumper opened his mouth to shout.

"*Gruu-mph!*" His mouth was suddenly full of teddy; Shaun had shoved Timmy's toy in Trumper's face, forcing his head back out of the horse's bottom.

Over his shoulder, Shaun bleated at Bitzer. They had to leave: *fast*!

Bitzer stamped on the pedals. The pantomime horse began to move away. But it was carrying the Farmer, a sheepdog and an entire flock of sheep. The weight slowed it down. Shaun groaned as he peered out through the horse's bum. Shouting at the horse to stop, Trumper was in hot pursuit, and it wouldn't take long for him to catch up. Shaun looked around desperately for anything that might help. His gaze fell on a fire extinguisher. Bitzer had insisted on bringing safety equipment, just in case.

Shaun grabbed the extinguisher and forced its nozzle out of the horse's backside. Squeezing his eyes closed, he pulled the release trigger.

In a cloud of horrible-smelling chemicals, the horse shot forward into the night.

Coughing in a cloud of foam, Trumper raised his Taser, flicking the switch and pulling the trigger at the same time. Crackling with power, an electrified claw zipped after the farting horse, trailing a long wire behind it.

The shot missed and ricocheted, tangling the wire around the horse's legs as Trumper gave chase. With a curse, he grabbed at the claw's wire.

It was a mistake.

Electricity burned into his hand. The air around him snapped and fizzled. His hair stood on end, smoking.

The panto horse zoomed away, dragging a screaming Trumper behind. On its back, the Farmer lolled this way and that while the sheep tried their best to keep him upright.

In his dreams, the Farmer sighed with pleasure at the lovely massage he was getting.

Bitzer yanked on the steering wheel, but the horse was out of control. The Flock yelped as they crashed through a wooden fence, towing Trumper behind.

A second later, the Animal Containment Officer burst through the wrecked fence, still holding onto the wire, with two planks stuck to his feet like skis. His scream became louder as he was pulled up a ramp, then abruptly stopped as he tipped over the edge and dropped into the jaws of a building site earth-mover.

Sheep cheered as Trumper disappeared, then turned to peer down the road as Bitzer whuffed in excitement. Up ahead, beneath yellow streetlights, was the old caravan, battered and crumpled, and abandoned in a lay-by at the side of the road. Bitzer pulled the handlebars round, steering towards it. Behind him, sheep released tattered clothes they had found under the arches and tied to the horse. Trousers and shirts and underwear puffed out like parachutes.

The pantomime horse slowed, and came to rest at the side of the caravan.

CHAPTER THIRTEEN

PEERING AROUND NERVOUSLY for any sign of Trumper, the sheep climbed out of the horse. The Animal Containment Officer was nowhere to be seen. Hooves gently lifted the Farmer, while others pulled open the caravan's door. When the Farmer was safely snuggled up under a blanket, the sheep scouted the gardens of houses lining the road. A few moments later, they returned with a borrowed washing line, which was quickly tied to the caravan's tow bar and then to the back bumper of a bus idling at a stop nearby.

Sighing with relief, the sheep clambered into the caravan. Ahead, the bus pulled away in a cloud of exhaust fumes. The caravan jerked and began rolling. Squashed against the back window, sheep faces peered at the road as Trumper finally appeared, smoking and battered, the Taser still gripped in one grimy hand.

The sheep waved at him as the caravan trundled away.

A moment later, Shaun heard a *thunk* and a rattling sound. He peered through the window again. Trumper had disappeared, but his Taser was dragging along, attached to the caravan by its long wire. Shaun grinned as the wire snapped, leaving the horrible machine lying in the road. Trumper must have tried one last time to grab the sheep, but he hadn't been able to run fast enough to keep up.

The caravan swayed and wobbled along behind the bus, city streets gradually giving way to trees and rolling fields. Slowly, the roads became narrower until the bus was finally rumbling along a country lane. Up ahead, Shaun spotted a familiar gate. Leaning out the front window, he bleated back at the Flock.

The sheep jumped together in unison, bouncing the caravan and unhitching it from the bus. The caravan slowed, one wheel bouncing off a rock to send it squeaking up a farm track. At exactly the spot where it had started, the caravan rolled to a gentle stop.

Sheep bleated in horror as it began to roll backwards again. They were headed back to the city!

A moment later, the bull heaved the caravan back into its usual place. Cheers burst from the caravan as the door flew open. The Flock, Bitzer and Slip had arrived safely at Mossy Bottom Farm! The animals carried the Farmer out, lowered him into the wheelbarrow and wheeled him towards the farmhouse. Shaun smiled. When the Farmer woke up in his own bed, Mr X would be completely forgotten.

Behind them, a hand appeared from beneath the caravan.

None of the animals noticed.

* * *

In the farmhouse, two pigs sat on the sofa flicking through a cookery book. Spotting a dish that looked tasty, one of them ripped the picture out and stuffed it in his mouth.

Squeee! A pig glanced out of the farmhouse window and squealed in shock. It was the Farmer, and he was headed straight for the house! The pig looked round in horror. While the Farmer had been away, the place had – quite literally – become a pigsty. Food and pig poo had been trodden into the carpet and splattered on the ceiling, chairs were overturned, and a partied-out pig was asleep in the Farmer's bathtub.

Squeeee! *Squeee! SQUEEEEEEEE!*

The farmhouse erupted as squealing pigs leapt to tidy the mess they'd made.

One furiously washed a pile of dirty dishes while another dumped a bowl of popcorn into the open mouth of a third pig. Another wiped a cloth over a moustache he'd drawn on a photo of the Farmer. Ink smeared over the picture, making it look even worse. In desperation, the pig hurriedly redrew the moustache.

Seconds later, the pigs fled out of the back door. With a final glance over his shoulder at the gleaming farmhouse, the last one out carefully wiped trotter prints from the door handle and pulled it closed behind him.

In the farmyard at the front of the house, the Flock had almost finished dressing the Farmer in his own clothes. A sheep lifted a Wellington boot and slipped it onto the

Farmer's foot, then stopped as he heard a shocked bleat.

Slip growled. Bitzer blinked. Shaun's jaw fell open. No, it couldn't be…

The rest of the Flock fell silent.

Standing in the distance, silhouetted against the moon with a scythe in his hand, was the unmistakable figure of Animal Containment Officer Trumper.

Shaun bleated in shock. The sound broke the silence. Sheep picked up the wheel-barrow and fled for the nearest hiding place – the small tool shed where the Farmer kept his clippers. Bitzer banged the door shut behind them, slamming bolts and latches, and locking the door. For good measure, he swallowed the key.

The animals of Mossy Bottom Farm

cowered in the dark as heavy boots stomped around the shed. The window's view of the moon vanished as Trumper wrapped the small building in crime-scene tape. They were trapped.

A few seconds later, Shaun heard the unmistakable sound of the Farmer's tractor wheezing and coughing to life. The sound came closer and closer until, with a loud *thump*, the tractor hit the shed.

Trumper shifted gears.

The engine strained.

Animals tumbled, bleating in fear as the shed fell on its side. Outside, the tractor's engine roared louder as Trumper began to half push, half roll the wooden shed across the meadow in the direction of the old quarry. The Farmer's head fell on Shirley.

Muttering happily in his sleep, he nestled into her thick fleece, dreaming of soft pillows.

Shaun gulped as the shed lurched and rolled across the meadow. The quarry was deep, with sheer rocky cliffs for walls. If Trumper pushed them into it no one would survive. If only the Farmer...

The Farmer! thought Shaun, as everybody was tossed around the shed as if they were in a huge washing machine. If anyone could help them now it was the Farmer. If only he remembered who he really was.

Reaching out a hoof, Shaun tried shaking him awake. The Farmer grumbled in his sleep and burrowed deeper into Shirley's fleece. Animals shouted in his ear, poking and nudging him. Still the Farmer slept on. Shaun gritted his teeth.

There was nothing else for it. If the Farmer couldn't be woken by normal methods, he would have to try something extreme. He scooped up a hoof-ful of old manure and held it to the Farmer's nose.

The shed came to a stop as it hit the wire fence surrounding the quarry. Metal screeched and twanged, but didn't break. Shaun heard Trumper curse, loudly. Then wood crunched, and the shed began to rise. Sheep shrieked. Trumper was using the tractor's grabbing claw to lift the whole shed over the deep, rocky pit. Any moment now, they'd fall and splat against the ground...

The Farmer's nose twitched at the foul smell underneath it. His eyelids fluttered. The sheep and Bitzer crowded round, bleating and whuffing loudly. Slowly, the

Farmer's eyes opened. For a second, he stared at the sea of frightened faces above him, then he screamed. He'd had a dreadful day – waking up in hospital, lost in the city, working hard at the salon – and now he was being held hostage by a gang of lunatic creatures.

The animals crowded closer, pleading in yelps and bleats for him to remember who he really was. With another screech, he struggled away from them, making the shed rock dangerously. Reaching out to support himself, the Farmer found himself clutching an old photograph. Without thinking, he looked at it.

The photo showed a group of young sheep, and a puppy. He peered closer, confused. At the centre of the photo, grinning broadly, was a man who looked like a younger version of himself.

The Farmer blinked as his memories returned in a rush. It *was* him. And these were *his* animals. This was his shed. *This* was where he was supposed to be. Not shearing people in a Big City salon. *Here*. On his farm. His lip wobbled. With a jolt, he realized how much he had missed the Flock, and Bitzer, and Mowermouth, and even the pigs and ducks.

A tear rolled down the Farmer's face.

Wood creaked alarmingly. Outside, the tractor's engine groaned, lifting the shed into position.

The Farmer stood up, a commanding figure in thick glasses, and looked round at the scared animals. An angry frown crossed his face. Whatever was frightening them, he would soon put a stop to it.

In one stride, he crossed to the door and pushed against it. Trumper's tape held it firmly in place. Grunting, the Farmer put his shoulder to it and heaved.

Tape snapped.

The door burst open.

Angrily, the Farmer stepped outside … and shrieked as he dropped into a dark abyss, only to jerk to a bouncing stop as a loop of crime-scene tape tangled around his ankle.

The animals crowded around the door, watching in horror as the Farmer dangled below them. Bitzer whuffed. The tape was straining to breaking point. They had to do something.

Hooves clamped around Bitzer's ankles and lowered him into the dark. He reached out to the Farmer, just a second too late.

With a faint ripping sound, the plastic tape snapped. The Farmer flailed blindly in the darkness, and grabbed onto Bitzer's ears. Above Bitzer, a chain of sheep swung from the open door of the shed.

Shaun gulped. The sheep couldn't hang on for ever, and Trumper could drop the whole shed into the quarry at any moment. It was up to him to save everyone. Teeth chattering, he crawled out from the shed and onto the tractor's arm. At the end of it sat Trumper, his hair sticking up crazily, smears of dirt and soot across his face.

With a bleat, Shaun threw himself at the Animal Containment Officer just as he reached for the lever that would release the tractor's grabber.

Trumper screamed as a sheep suddenly flew out of the dark, straight at him.

Shaun's scrabbling hooves pressed a button. Windscreen cleaning liquid jetted out and hit Trumper in the eyes. Hitting *that* button had worked so well, Shaun immediately tried another. Windscreen wipers slapped Trumper's face again and again.

With a howl of pure fury, the animal cop lurched at Shaun, grabbing handfuls of fleece.

Shaun struggled, but Trumper gripped him with all his strength. Roaring with victory, he held the sheep above his head, stepped down from the tractor and flung Shaun into the dark hole of the quarry.

Shaun managed a horrified, yelping bleat. Then he was falling.

He squeezed his eyes closed.

It was all over.

A strong hand gripped him. Shaun's eyes fluttered open. He bleated weakly as he looked up into a face that was frowning with worry.

Shaun bleated: *I'm OK.*

Relieved, the Farmer held tightly onto Shaun's hoof while still clutching Bitzer's stretched ear with his spare hand.

Hearing a growl, Shaun glanced back towards Trumper. The Animal Containment Officer was now hopping around in agony. Attached to his foot was the tiny Slip. She growled and sank her teeth in as hard as she could, making Trumper scream.

Hopping and swearing, he bent over to pull the small dog off his foot. Ripped trousers strained over his bottom, revealing his underwear – *red* underwear.

Shaun's eyes widened as he heard a rumble of hooves in the darkness, and a bellow of rage.

With a shriek, Trumper flew through the air, legs windmilling wildly and his hands clutching his backside where the bull's horns had ripped new holes in his pants.

Splat.

Cheers and laughs split the air as Animal Containment Officer Trumper landed head-first into a steaming pile of fresh manure.

The bull scratched a front hoof in the dirt in satisfaction of a job well done.

CHAPTER FOURTEEN

BITZER WHUFFED, flapping at sheep slowly making their way back towards the barn. Shaun trailed over, brightening when he found himself standing next to the sheepdog. It had been a difficult day, but everything had turned out OK, and it had been fun, sort of. Grinning, he punched Bitzer on the arm.

Bitzer gave him a look, which turned into a snigger. He punched Shaun back.

153

A second later, they were hugging. With a cough of embarrassment, Shaun finally let his friend go. Looking out over his beloved farm, he yawned and stretched. It was almost dawn – time to turn in.

A moment later he stumbled to a halt, surprised to find a note fluttering under a stone by the barn. Curiously, he picked it up, and read. *"Woof, woof, bark, woof."* Shaun's eyes widened. Slip's note said she was happy her new friends had made it home, but it wasn't the place for her. It wasn't *her* home.

Shaun sniffed, a lump in his throat. Slip had become a friend. She was welcome to stay on the farm. Maybe the Farmer would adopt her. Waving the note, he dashed off in the direction of the road, arriving just in time to see Slip lit up by the headlights of an oncoming bus.

The bus screeched to a halt. The door hissed open. The female bus driver peered down as Slip clambered aboard. Shaun couldn't help noticing that the driver's face was a little bit lopsided, and that the smile that lit up her face when she spotted the little dog was crooked. Slip's face, too, broke into a grin as she looked up at the bus driver. A second later, she was lifted into the air. Shyly, she licked the woman's face and was rewarded with a squeal of happiness.

It was love at first sight.

As the bus rumbled away towards the city, Slip waved goodbye.

A tear in his eye, Shaun waved back.

* * *

As the sun rose, a bird tweeted on the branch of a tree outside the barn. The cockerel, miffed that he had been beaten to it, stood up on a gate post and filled his lungs. A second later, a loud crow echoed around Mossy Bottom Farm. In the barn, Shaun grinned up at his old friend the useless spider, and sprang to his feet. Throwing the window open, he took a deep breath of farm air and the smell from the pigsty. He was *home*, and it was a beautiful spring day.

Bitzer sat up, hit his head on the kennel ceiling, and cricked his neck back into place. He tucked his newspaper under his arm and set off for his favourite tree. As he crossed the farmyard, he gave a tiny skip.

With a cheerful *ding-a-ling-a-ling*, the Farmer's alarm clock went off in his bedroom. The Farmer thumped it and sat up, scratching his head in confusion. He turned to look out the window. Everything was fine. He was at home and the sun was shining. It must have all been just a very strange dream...

Chuckling, the Farmer jumped out of bed and tore a page from the calendar: "THURSDAY".

A few moments later, the farmhouse door burst open. Grabbing it before it could squash Bitzer against the wall, the Farmer rumpled the sheepdog's ears with an affectionate "heh heh" and set off for the barn. For a second, Bitzer grinned in surprised delight, and then the door slammed open again, squashing him against the wall. Without a backwards glance, a partied-out pig – who had been asleep in the bathtub – scurried away.

The barn doors were thrown open. Grinning, Shaun shoved the other sheep aside and appeared front and centre while Bitzer held up the clipboard holding the day's schedule.

At the sight of the clipboard, Shaun's heart sank a little. He sighed. So much for a day off.

At the sight of the schedule, a horrified shudder ran through the Farmer.

Bitzer blinked up at him, hesitating. Then he lowered the clipboard. After staring at the schedule for half a second, the sheepdog ripped it off, scrunched it into a ball and tossed it over his shoulder.

Mowermouth watched as it rolled to his feet, and then ate it.

A cheer rang out from the barn. The Farmer patted Bitzer on the head.

With a happy sigh, the Farmer flopped into an armchair and picked up a steaming mug of tea while he flicked the television on. The news was on. A man suffering memory loss had disappeared from hospital. The Farmer tutted, then shot forward, spitting tea as a photo of the missing man appeared. It was *him*!

First published 2015 by Walker Entertainment
An imprint of
Walker Books Ltd
87 Vauxhall Walk
London SE11 5HJ

4 6 8 10 9 7 5

This book was typeset in ITC Cheltenham.

Printed and bound in Great Britain by Clays Ltd, St Ives plc

British Library Cataloguing in Publication Data: a catalogue record for this
book is available from the British Library

ISBN 978-1-4063-5964-0

www.walker.co.uk